MEET CARLY AND CARTOKA!

Based on the episode
"Carly and Cartoka"

Ready-to-Read

Simon Spotlight
New York London Toronto Sydney New Delhi

PJ Masks © 2022 FrogBox/Ent. One UK Ltd/Hasbro.
Based on the original books by Romuald *Les Pyjamasques* © 2007 first published in
France by Gallimard Jeunesse.

SIMON SPOTLIGHT
An imprint of Simon & Schuster Children's Publishing Division
1230 Avenue of the Americas, New York, New York 10020
This Simon Spotlight edition August 2022
Adapted by Maria Le from the series PJ Masks
For information about special discounts for bulk purchases, please contact Simon
& Schuster Special Sales at 1-866-506-1949 or business@simonandschuster.com.
Manufactured in the United States of America 0722 LAK
10 9 8 7 6 5 4 3 2 1
ISBN 978-1-6659-1914-2 (hc)
ISBN 978-1-6659-1913-5 (pb)
ISBN 978-1-6659-1915-9 (ebook)

Amaya, Connor, and Greg
are walking home
from school.
"Look!" says Greg.

Someone has taken

all the parts

from the cars.

This is a job
for the PJ Masks!

Amaya becomes Owlette!

Connor becomes Catboy!

Greg becomes Gekko!

They are the PJ Masks!

Something zooms
across the street.
What could it be?

Owlette, Catboy, and
Gekko chase after it.

A car spins to a stop.
Two strangers jump out.

"We are Carly and
Cartoka. This is
our Flashcar!" they say.

Carly drives the Flashcar
and zooms away.

Catboy tries to chase
the Flashcar. The
Cat-Car crashes into the
Owl Glider and Gekko-Mobile!

Cartoka uses the Gigantogarage to steal the Owl Glider and Gekko-Mobile!

The new Flashcar skids out
of the Gigantogarage.
Cartoka took the PJ vehicle
parts for the Flashcar.

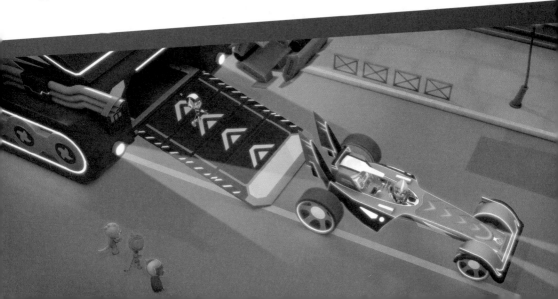

The twins zoom away in their high-tech racecar. Catboy chases after them, but the Flashcar is faster.

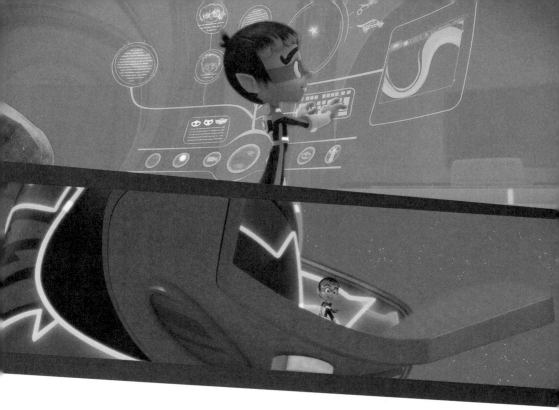

Carly and Cartoka beat
the PJ Masks to HQ and
steal all the PJ vehicles!

The PJ Sub, PJ Seeker,
and PJ Rovers are gone!
Catboy chases after the
Flashcar in his Cat-Car.

"Wait!" says Gekko.
"We should work
as a team!" says Owlette.
Catboy speeds away.

He goes faster and faster.

The road starts glowing!

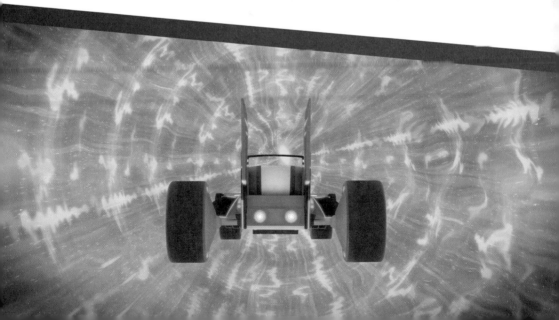

There is a bright flash!
The Cat-Car and Flashcar
jump into Zoomzania.

"Only the fastest cars can go to Zoomzania!" says Cartoka.

Catboy loses control

of the Cat-Car.

Carly and Cartoka

steal it, too!

Catboy needs to get back to his friends. But how will he get there without his Cat-Car?

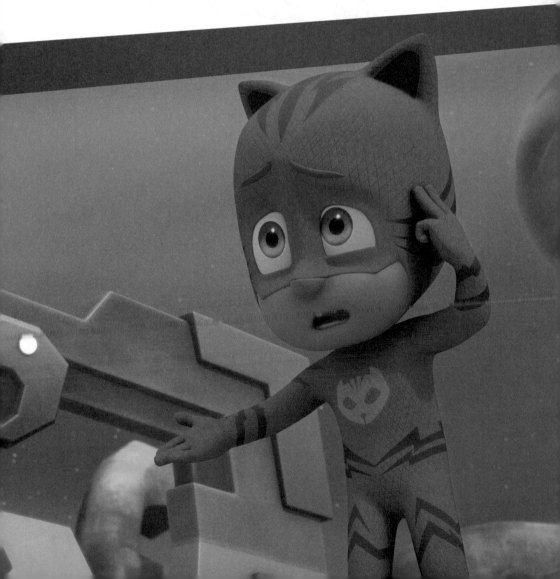

"My PJ Pals. They need me.
And I need them.
Time to be a hero!"
says Catboy.

He has an idea.
Catboy still has
Super Cat Speed!

Catboy runs faster
than he has ever before.
"Super Cat Speed!" he says.
Catboy escapes Zoomzania.

Catboy races into HQ. "I am sorry for leaving my friends behind," says Catboy.

"We are glad
you are back,"
says Owlette.

Blue, red, and green
rays of light shine
from the PJ Crystal.

The lights flash.

Power Lizard,

Cat Stripe King, and

Eagle Owl appear!

The PJ Masks race out
into the night on their
new animal partners.

"No fair! Those do not have wheels!" says Carly. The twins speed away in their Flashcar.

PJ Masks all shout hooray!
Because in the night
they saved the day!